An I Can Read Book™

Marvin One Too Many

story by Katherine Paterson

pictures by Jane Clark Brown

HarperCollins*Publishers*

ER

HarperCollins®, 📖®, and I Can Read Book®
are trademarks of HarperCollins Publishers Inc.

Marvin One Too Many
Text copyright © 2001 by Minna Murra, Inc.
Illustrations copyright © 2001 by Jane Clark Brown
Printed in the U.S.A. All rights reserved.
www.harperchildrens.com

Library of Congress Cataloging-in-Publication Data
Paterson, Katherine.
    Marvin one too many / by Katherine Paterson ; pictures by Jane Clark Brown.
        p.   cm. — (I can read book)
    Summary: Marvin cannot read, but he eventually learns to with some help from his father.
ISBN 0-06-028769-1 — ISBN 0-06-028770-5 (lib. bdg.)
    [1. Reading—Fiction.   2. Schools—Fiction.   3. Fathers and sons—Fiction.]   I. Brown,
Jane Clark, ill.   II. Title.   III. Series.
PZ7.P273 Map   2001   00-046128
[E]—dc21   CIP
                                                                              AC

1   2   3   4   5   6   7   8   9   10
❖
First Edition

For
Barbara Hughes Thompson
and
Hazel Bowman Horton
for whom no child was ever
one too many
with love and gratitude
—K.P.

For Anne Putnam Clark
Wise teacher of many
and loving mother of four
—J.C.B.

Marvin Gates was scared.

His new school was too big.

He got lost.

His sister, May, had to help him.

"You made me late on the first day,"

she said.

Marvin felt like crying,

but he didn't cry.

"Here is your class," said May.

"See? Your teacher looks nice!"

Marvin felt better.

Then the teacher said: "One more?

That is one too many!"

Marvin felt terrible.

He thought his teacher

didn't like him.

Marvin saw cards everywhere,

even on the teacher.

"I am Ms. Brown," said the teacher.

She pointed to her card.

"Brrrrr-OW-na!"

"What is the matter?" asked Marvin.

"Are you cold?"

Ms. Brown laughed.

All the children laughed, too—

except Marvin.

He felt like one too many.

Ms. Brown pointed to another card.

"Can anyone read this card?"

"I can," said a girl.

"It says 'Mary.'

Mary is my name."

"Good," said Ms. Brown.

"Mmmma-ree can read her name."

10

"Me too! Me too!" everyone yelled—

except Marvin.

He didn't have a card.

He was one too many.

The next day Ms. Brown said:

"Find your card and sit down."

"Do I have a card?" asked Marvin.

"Yes," said Ms. Brown.

"Today you have a card."

Marvin felt happy.

He saw M for Marvin.

He ran and sat down.

"No," said a girl.

"You are not Mary.

I am Mary."

All the children laughed—

except Marvin.

Every day things got worse.

Everyone could read all the cards—

except Marvin.

He was always one too many.

Marvin wanted to tell Mom and Dad,

but he didn't want to worry them.

"Here is a note for home,"

said Ms. Brown.

"Your parents must sign this note.

They must read with you every day."

How could Mom and Dad do that?

They were much too busy.

Ms. Brown did not understand.

She did not know about dairy farms.

"Will you read with me?"

Marvin asked May.

"No," said May.

"I have too much homework."

Marvin tore up Ms. Brown's note.

19

The other children made fun of him.

"You can't read," Mary said.

"Maybe his mom and dad can't read," said Joe.

Marvin felt like crying,

but he didn't cry.

He hit Joe instead.

Ms. Brown was not happy.

"You're mad because you can't read," said Mary.

"Reading is dumb," said Marvin.

Soon everyone was reading books—
except Marvin.

"Choose a book," Ms. Brown said.

"We have lots of good books."

"Books are dumb," said Marvin.

Marvin wanted the snow to come.

He wanted a huge storm.

Then there would be no school.

24

At last a big storm did come.

Marvin was very happy.

He could stay home.

At home he was not one too many.

Dad was worried about the storm.

"If we lose power," he said,

"how will we milk the cows?"

"If the road is too bad," said Mom,

"how can the truck

pick up the milk?"

"My class has a field trip tomorrow.

Now we can't go," May said.

How could Marvin tell them

the storm was all his fault?

He felt like crying,

but he didn't cry.

27

"Okay, Marvin," said May.

"Do you want to play school?"

Marvin hated school,

but he wanted May to feel better.

"Here are some cards," said May.

"Now, what does this card say?"

"I don't know," said Marvin sadly.

"Marvin! It's your favorite thing!"

said May.

On the back was the picture of a cow.

"Cuh-OW!" said May.

"Are you hurt?" asked Marvin.

"No," May said.

"Look! Cuh-OW. Cow."

She showed him another card.

"What does this card say?"

Marvin shook his head.

On the back of the card was a cat.

"Cat?" asked Marvin.

"No," said May. "Me-OW.

See the OW in me-OW?

Just like the OW in cow.

See?"

Marvin didn't see.

"Reading is dumb," he said.

Mom and Dad came in.

They were covered with snow.

"It's snowing hard," said Mom.

"I hope the snowplow gets here."

"I hope the power stays on,"

said Dad.

Just then all the lights went out.

Mom and Dad were very worried.

It was all Marvin's fault.

Marvin felt like crying,

and he did cry.

"What's the matter?" asked Dad.

"It's all my fault," said Marvin.

"I wanted a big storm

so I wouldn't have to go to school."

36

"Marvin, the storm is not your fault,"

said Dad.

"What is the problem at school?"

"Reading," said Marvin.

"Everyone can read—except me."

"Yes," Dad said. "That is very hard.

Did you know I was the last one

to read in my class, too?"

Marvin couldn't believe it.

His dad was very smart.

He knew all about cows and trucks.

"Yes," said Dad. "I was the last one."

"Reading is dumb," said Marvin.

"No," said Dad. "Reading is great.

It takes more time for some of us.

You'll catch on soon, I know."

Marvin felt a little better.

"Will you read to me?" he asked.

"Sure," said Dad.

May found a funny poem about a cow

for Dad to read.

Dad put his finger under each word.

"'I never saw a purple cow,

I never hope to see one.

But I can tell you anyhow,

I'd rather see than be one.'"

"OW!" said Marvin.

"Are you hurt?" asked Dad.

"No!" said Marvin. "See? OW!

Cuh-OW. COW!"

"You are reading!" said Dad.

"You read 'cow'!"

"I love cows," said Marvin.

"'Cow' is my favorite word.

Did you know my name moos

just like a cow?" Marvin said.

"How can Marvin moo?" asked Dad.

"Mmmmmmar-vin!" said Marvin.

"You're right, Marvin!

The M moos, just like a cow."

Just then all the lights came on.

Soon they heard the snowplow.

"Yippee!" said Marvin.

"Tomorrow I can tell Ms. Brr-OW-na

about all Mmmmmar-vin's cuh-OWs!"

"Tell Ms. Brr-OW-na for me

that we will read together every night.

Guys who take a little longer

need to stick together," said Dad.

47

And that is h-OW

Mmmmmar-vin started reading and

stopped being Marvin one too many.